A Random House PICTUREBACK® Book

Random House 🏠 New York

© 2018 Viacom International Inc., and Spin Master PAW Productions Inc. All rights reserved. Published in the United States by Random House Children's Books, a division of Penguin Random House LLC, 1745 Broadway, New York, NY 10019, and in Canada by Penguin Random House Canada Limited, Toronto. The stories contained in this collection were originally published separately by Random House Books for Young Readers in slightly different form as *Holiday Helpers!* in 2016, and by Golden Books in slightly different form as *Santa's Christmas Genies* in 2016, *A Monster Machine Christmas* in 2016, and *The Knight Before Christmas* in 2018. Pictureback, Random House, and the Random House colophon are registered trademarks of Penguin Random House LLC. PAW Patrol and all related titles, logos, and characters are trademarks of Spin Master Ltd. Nickelodeon, Nick Jr., Shimmer and Shine, Blaze and the Monster Machines, Nella the Princess Knight, and all related titles and logos are trademarks of Viacom International Inc.

rhcbooks.com

ISBN 978-0-525-58067-6

MANUFACTURED IN CHINA

10 9 8 7 6 5 4 3 2

CONTENTS

HOLIDAY HELPERS!

By Tex Huntley

Adapted from the teleplay "The Pups Save Christmas"
by Ursula Ziegler-Sullivan

Illustrated by Harry Moore

It was the day before Christmas, and the PAW Patrol was busy decorating the giant tree outside the Lookout.

"I love Christmas!" Zuma exclaimed. "I can't wait for Santa to get here."

Skye soared to the top of the tree and placed a shiny star there. "Now we know Santa will find us!" she declared.

But that night, as Santa was making his deliveries, there was a terrible storm. His sleigh was rocked by winds. Bags of gifts fell out, and the Magic Christmas Star that made the sleigh fly was lost! Santa made an emergency landing in the snow.

Santa called Ryder and told him about the missing gifts and star. "I need you and the PAW Patrol to help me save Christmas!"
"Save Christmas?" Ryder gasped. "Us?"

"I thought there was no job too big and no pup too small," Santa said.
Ryder nodded. "You're right, Santa. We'll do everything we can to help!"

Ryder told the pups about Santa's problems. He needed the entire team's help if they were going to save Christmas.

Ryder said they would use Rubble's shovel to dig the sleigh out of the snow, and Rocky would fix any damages.

Skye, Zuma, and Marshall would search for the missing gifts.

9

"And, Chase," Ryder said, "I need your megaphone and net to help round up Santa's reindeer."
"Chase is on the case!" Chase yipped.

The PAW Patrol
was ready to roll.

Ryder and the pups found Santa's sleigh
buried in the snow.
"Stand back!" Rubble said. "I'll dig it out."
He extended the shovel from his Pup Pack
and went to work.

After the snow had been cleared away, Rocky raised the sleigh with his truck and Ryder inspected the damage. The crash had broken one of the sleigh's runners. Luckily, Rocky had an old ski that could replace it.

Meanwhile, Skye searched for Santa's missing gifts. Her searchlight scanned the dark trees.

"I see a bag," she reported to Chase and Marshall.

Marshall extended the ladder on his truck and climbed up. He reached for the bag—and slipped!

Marshall and the bag tumbled down.
Chase quickly launched a net that caught
the sack. Marshall landed in the soft snow.
"I'm good," he said with a smile.

Once the pups had found all the gifts, it was time to deliver them. Skye swooped through the chilly air and dropped a bag down the chimney of Katie's Pet Parlor.

"Bull's-eye!" she exclaimed.

Meanwhile, Marshall tumbled down Mayor Goodway's chimney.
"Bwok!" said Chickaletta.

"Shhh. Don't wake the mayor," Marshall whispered as he
slipped a gift under the tree. He even had a gift-wrapped ear of
corn for Chickaletta.

At the same time, Zuma guided his hovercraft to Cap'n Turbot's Lighthouse. Suddenly, Wally the Walrus popped out of the water and blocked his way.

Zuma had a gift for Wally. "Merry Christmas, dude!" Wally barked his thanks and moved aside.

Over at Farmer Yumi's Farm, Ryder, Rocky, and Rubble were searching for the Magic Christmas Star. They didn't find anything . . . until Ryder pointed into the night sky.

Bettina the cow was flying through the air—with the Christmas star stuck to her side!

Ryder coaxed her down with some hay and got the star back.

Meanwhile, Chase had found Santa's reindeer.

"ATTENTION, ALL REINDEER!" he announced into his megaphone. "PLEASE MOVE FORWARD IN AN ORDERLY FASHION!"

They followed Chase back to Santa's sleigh.

"My sleigh looks perfect!" Santa exclaimed.
"Except for one missing piece," Ryder said,
handing the Magic Christmas Star to Santa.
Santa hung the star on the front of his sleigh.

While the pups loaded the gifts onto
Santa's sleigh, Skye took the reins playfully.
"I've always wanted to sit here. Now dash
away, dash away, dash away, all!"

Suddenly, the reindeer leaped into the air
and pulled the sleigh with them. The PAW
Patrol zoomed through the starry sky!

When the sleigh landed, it was time for Santa to leave.
"Whenever you're in trouble, just 'ho, ho, ho' for help!"
Ryder said as he and the pups waved goodbye to Santa.

The next morning, the pups wanted to open their gifts, but first they gave a present to Ryder. It was a giant . . . bone!

"It smells delicious," Chase said, licking his lips.

"It's perfect!" Ryder exclaimed. "But I'll tell you what, pups—you can have it. Merry Christmas, everyone!"

Shimmer and Shine™

Santa's Christmas Genies

By Hollis James
Adapted from the teleplay "Santa's Little Genies" by Sindy Boveda Spackman
Illustrated by Mattia Francesco Laviosa

It was the day before Christmas, and Leah and Zac were writing letters to Santa.

"All I want for Christmas is a canoe," Zac said.

"I'm asking Santa for snow on Christmas," Leah said.

Zac wanted to go home to make room for his canoe, so Leah offered to mail his letter for him.

The mail truck arrived, and Leah ran to meet it. But when she returned to her house, she saw Zac's letter on the ground. She'd dropped it! Now her friend wouldn't get his Christmas canoe.

"If only I had a way to get this to Santa before Christmas," she said. Then she realized she did—her magical genies-in-training, Shimmer and Shine!

She called for them, and they appeared in a *poof* of sparkles with their pets, Tala and Nahal.

Shimmer wished everyone to Santa's workshop at the North Pole. The elves invited them in and gave them hot chocolate so they could warm up.

"This Santa fella really knows how to live," said Shine.

Leah and the genies even met Santa. He gave them a tour of the workshop. They saw where the Christmas letters went and where the toys were made.

At the end of the tour, Santa said, "I hope you enjoyed visiting my workshop." "We did," said Leah, shivering. "But I wish you lived someplace warmer!" Shine immediately cast a spell.

Whoosh! Santa was whisked away to a tropical island.

When the elves heard that Santa was gone, they started to panic.

"I wish these elves would calm down!" said Leah.

Shimmer was happy to help. She cast a spell that sent the elves into a deep sleep.

Now Santa was gone and the elves were napping. Who would get the gifts ready for Christmas and deliver them?

It was up to Leah, Shimmer, and Shine!

The genies went to work using
magic to finish the rest of the toys.

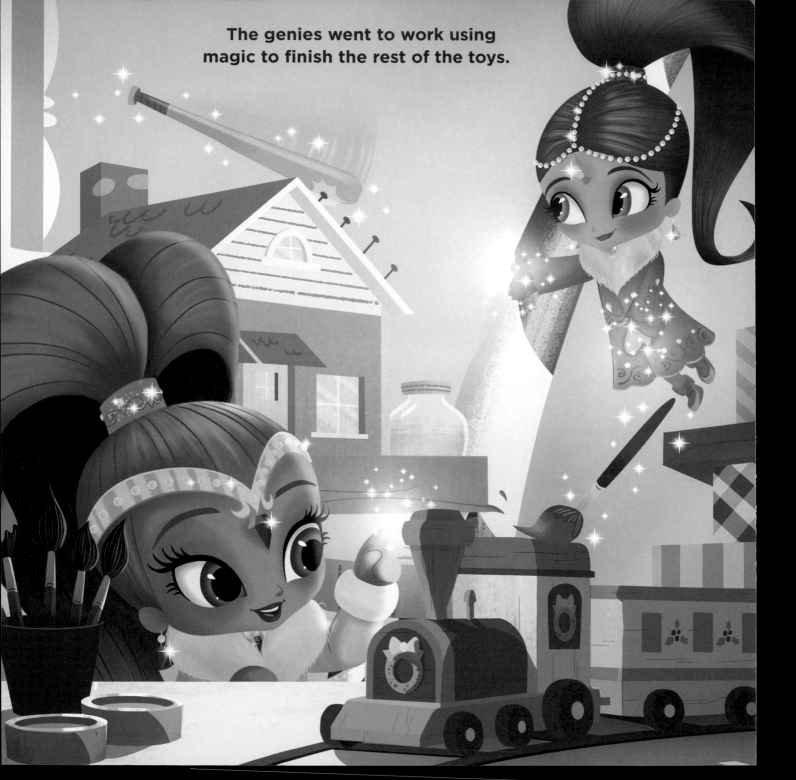

Shimmer and Shine loaded the toys onto Santa's sleigh, but they weren't sure how to start it. Shine pressed something. It was the Santa-tracking button! The reindeer leapt into the air and flew Leah and her friends straight to the beach where Santa was stranded.

The sleigh crashed to a stop in the sand. Leah and her friends tried to move the sleigh, but it was stuck!

"If only we had something else that Santa could fly," said Leah.

Poof! Santa was back in his red suit and perched on a magic carpet.

"Ho, ho, ho!" he exclaimed. "It's time to save Christmas!"

Flying from house to house, Leah, Shimmer, and Shine helped Santa deliver presents all around the world.

When the gifts had been delivered,
Santa took Leah home.
"Santa, thank you so much for
everything," said Leah.

"You're welcome," Santa replied. But he still had one more gift—he made it snow! A blanket of white quickly covered the street.

"It's snowing for Christmas morning!" Leah exclaimed.

Santa and the genies flew away just as Zac ran up.
He was carrying something really big.

"I got my canoe!" he announced. "And you got
what you wanted, too, Leah!"

The genies and Santa returned to the tropical island and freed his sleigh from the sand. To thank them, Santa gave them a gift—a hot-chocolate maker! And they had a gift for him—a genie bottle!

"Now you can bring Christmas to Zahramay Falls!" Shine said.

Shimmer and Shine flew away on their magic carpet. They sang as they sailed out of sight: *"We saved the day with three merry wishes! Boom, Zahramay! We'll see you next Christmas!"*

By Frank Berrios
Adapted from the teleplay "Blaze Christmas" by Jeff Borkin
Illustrated by Dynamo Limited

It was Christmas Eve, and Blaze and AJ were helping Santa get ready for the big day.

"Santa's bag can hold presents for everyone in the world!" said AJ.

"My elves and I make sure we've got the perfect present for every boy and girl," said Santa. "Everyone should feel special on Christmas!"

The present meter on the bag showed that it was full.

"Ho, ho, ho! Now I've got Christmas presents for everyone!" chuckled Santa Claus.

Santa and his friends were so busy that no one noticed two uninvited guests.

"I want to look in Santa's bag and find *my* Christmas present," Crusher whispered to Pickle. But before he could find his gift, the bag began to roll away . . . with Crusher on top of it!

The bag rolled down a hill. It spilled open, and presents soared through the air in every direction!

"Don't worry, Santa," said AJ. "Those presents are out there somewhere."

"And AJ and I are going to find them!" added Blaze.

Crusher wanted to come, but he only wanted to find *his* gift.

"Just remember, Crusher," said Santa, "it's important that you help Blaze find *everyone's* present. Everyone should feel special on Christmas."

Blaze and Crusher raced off. Before long, they arrived at the ice-crystal caves.

"Hey, look up there!" said AJ. "It's a whole bunch of presents frozen in ice!"

Crusher tried to use a suction-cup bow and arrow to get the presents, but his toy arrow couldn't fly far enough to grab them.

Then Blaze had an idea. "Let's be engineers and build a *better* bow and arrow!"

Blaze and AJ worked together to make a giant bendy bow and an arrow with a big suction cup. Blaze aimed, hit the mark, and pulled the presents free from the ice! Crusher checked the bag, but none of the presents were his. The trio kept searching.

Soon Blaze and his friends spotted a pile of presents at the bottom of a very steep hill. But to get to the presents, they needed to jump over some giant candy canes.

"Let's build a sled with a turbojet engine!" said AJ.

"Woo-hoo! I'm a Turbo-Sled Monster Machine!" exclaimed Blaze. He took off with a burst down the candy-cane hill.

At the bottom, Crusher peered into the bag. "All these presents, and none of them are for me!"

The group continued on their journey to find the rest of the presents.

They came to Snowball Mountain,
which was shooting out giant snowballs!
"Let's make a really big water blaster!"
Blaze suggested.
AJ agreed. "Then we can blast those
snowballs!" he said.
They quickly got to work.

Water-blastin' Blaze blasted all the giant snowballs. When the Monster Machines reached the top of the mountain, Crusher checked the bag and found what he was looking for.

"I got my present!" he shouted with glee.

Suddenly, the ice on the mountaintop began to give way!

"Oh, no! Santa's bag is falling!" cried AJ.

"It's too heavy," said Blaze, struggling to save the presents. "I can't pull it up by myself."

Crusher remembered what Santa had said: *everyone* should feel special on Christmas. "If those presents fall and break," he said to himself, "no one will feel special on Christmas! I've got to save those presents!"

Crusher and Blaze pulled together—and saved the bag of gifts.

As Crusher and Blaze celebrated, Santa appeared!
"Look, Santa! We got all the presents!" said Crusher.
"That's wonderful!" said Santa. "Now we just need
some way to deliver them before it's too late."

"I can do it!" offered Blaze. "With Blazing Speed,
I can help you deliver the presents super fast!"
"Ho, ho, ho—that's it!" chuckled Santa.
"Blaze, you can be my sleigh tonight!"
Blaze quickly transformed into a super sleigh.

"Let's deliver some Christmas presents!" said super-sleigh Blaze. AJ, Santa, and Crusher hopped aboard. With a burst of Blazing Speed, they took off into the night sky.

With Blaze's amazing speed, Santa was able to deliver all the gifts in time for Christmas Day.

Everyone in Axle City waved and cheered. They knew they would have a very merry Christmas!

Nella
THE PRINCESS KNIGHT

The Knight Before Christmas

By David Lewman
Based on the teleplay by Jim Nolan
Illustrated by Monica Davila

"I love, love, LOVE Christmastime!" Nella said to her unicorn friend, Trinket.

It was Christmas Eve, and Nella and the whole royal family were busy decorating their tree and eating gingerbread knights.

Suddenly, they heard singing outside the castle.

Sir Garrett and Clod were singing Christmas carols!

The friends looked up to the sky and saw Santa.
He was being chased by the Frostbite Brothers!
They were three naughty ice dragons named
Freezy, Frozey, and Snowpuff.

The ice dragons stole Santa's bag of presents!
"I've got to help Santa!" Nella declared. "My heart
glows bright—it's time to be a Princess Knight!"

Nella, Sir Garrett, Trinket, and Clod chased the Frostbite Brothers. They cornered the ice dragons at the foot of a steep mountain.

The tricky brothers used their super-cold breath to make a frozen staircase—and escaped up the mountainside.

Nella and her friends started to climb the stairs.

But the dragons turned the staircase into a slide!

"WHOOAAA!" Nella and her friends cried as they slid down.

Nella shot a ribbon arrow into the top of the mountain. She and her friends climbed up!

Next, the dragons tried to stop Nella and her friends with a gigantic ice wall.

"Ha!" Snowpuff laughed. "Even a cool Princess Knight won't be able to get over an ice wall."

But Nella rode her shield like a snowboard and slid over the wall!

Nella and her friends caught the
Frostbite Brothers as they ran into a cave.
"Game over!" Nella said. "Give back
those presents!"
The dragons blew on the entrance and
created a door of solid ice.

Nella used her sword to carve a gigantic key.
"Come on, guys!" she called. "This is going to take all of us!"
Working together, the friends opened the door.

Inside the cave, Nella explained to the ice dragons that Christmas is more than just presents. "The best part," she said, "is we get to spend the whole day laughing and playing with all the people we love!"

"I never knew Christmas meant so much," said Snowpuff. "We're sorry, Nella."
Nella asked the dragons to celebrate Christmas with them—and the brothers happily agreed!

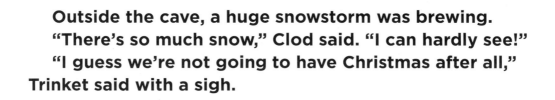

Outside the cave, a huge snowstorm was brewing.
"There's so much snow," Clod said. "I can hardly see!"
"I guess we're not going to have Christmas after all,"
Trinket said with a sigh.

"We'll take you!" Snowpuff said.
Freezy, Frozey, and Snowpuff made an ice sleigh.
Sir Garrett, Clod, and Trinket hopped in, and the sleigh
took off into the sky. Nella rode on Snowpuff's back,
her glowing sword lighting the way!

Nella returned the bag of presents to Santa. "We just might be able to get these presents to all the nice boys and girls and creatures in time for Christmas," Santa said.

But he needed everyone to help him—even the Frostbite Brothers!

Nella and the ice dragons helped deliver all the presents!
"All right!" Nella exclaimed. "Great job, everyone!"

On Christmas morning, as the villagers gathered around Castlehaven's Christmas tree, Santa flew his sleigh right into the town square.

"Thanks to Nella and her friends," he said, "everyone got their Christmas wishes!"

The villagers cheered and enjoyed a very merry day together.